THE PEOPLE OF
P·E·R·N ™
ROBIN WOOD

DEC	JAN 6			

THE PEOPLE OF
P·E·R·N ™
ROBIN WOOD

with text and introduction
by
Anne McCaffrey

THE
DONNING COMPANY
PUBLISHERS
NORFOLK / VIRGINIA BEACH

Distributed by
Schiffer Publishing Ltd.
1469 Morstein Road, WEst Chester, PA 13980

DEDICATION

I would like to dedicate this book to all those who helped me.

Anne, without whom there would be no book, and also no Pern! Thank you for your warmth and support, and for your endless patience answering all those questions, and working with me until we got everyone *right*.

Bill and Jody, for giving me my first chance to work with Anne, and for all your help with this project (especially the transcript).

Stan and Bev, for being willing to do this book.

David and Jean, my editors, for your help and understanding.

Stacia, Zack, Melody, Lee, Skip, Tay, Stephan, Leslie, Thanos, Gerri, Lovey, Jason and Elric, for posing for me. Notably Stacia, "Miss Pern 1988," who posed for all but two of the females, and whose face appears (slightly altered) only as Corana; and Zack, who posed for most of the males, and is Brand. Thank you all, I couldn't have done it without you.

Rhymer, Jim, Carol, Fritz, the Bungaloids and all the other fen that I have talked to at the conventions, for your enthusiasm and support, not to mention visits and meals when I was trapped in the studio.

And lastly, and most importantly, to my housemates, Elisa and Stephan, for putting up with long hours, my snappishness, the times that I got discouraged, and an apartment full of Grumtine, and returning stories, backrubs, and boundless faith in my abilities. You kept me on an even keel, and I can't thank you enough.

Thank you, as well, to all of you who are buying this book. I hope you enjoy owning, reading, and looking at it as much as I enjoyed painting it— for I did truly enjoy it, all those fourteen-hour days notwithstanding. I thank you, my cats thank you, and my landlord thanks you!

Have fun!!

Please write to the Donning Company for a free catalog of books of similar interest
  c/o Schiffer Publishing Ltd., distrubutor
  1469 Morstein Road, West Chester, PA 19380
  Tel. 215-696-1001.

Printed in the United States of America

CONTENTS

INTRODUCTION TO PERN

Anne McCaffrey

In what started as a *short* story to improve the public image of the much maligned "dragon," I wrote "Weyr Search," set on a planet orbiting the sun Rukbat which I located on the National Geographic Star Map in the lower left hand corner. One million words later, I'm not allowed to stop!

For those to whom such details matter, the chronological order of the books in Pern's history is: *Dragonsdawn, Moreta: Dragonlady of Pern, Dragonflight, Dragonquest*. Read *Dragonsong* and *Dragonsinger*, then the first two chapters of *The White Dragon, Dragondrums*, and the rest of *The White Dragon*. You will then have read them in sequence.

For those who wish to enter the Pern orbit more gently, read *Dragonflight* first (for it was the first book written), or *Dragonsong*.

When John W. Campbell, celebrated editor of *Analog Magazine*, accepted "Weyr Search" for publication, he asked me to suggest, in some way, that my characters had Terran origins. "It makes my readers more comfortable to know," he told me. Frankly, I didn't want to tie Pern down in any way to Terran origins. I wanted to shelter and protect this marvelous world from any intrusions. But the wise writer complied with John's suggestions. So I invented the prologue to Pern, which goes something like this:

When Mankind first discovered Pern, third planet of the sun Rukbat in the Sagittarian Sector, they paid little attention to the eccentric orbit of another satellite in the system.

Settling the new planet, adjusting to its differences, the colonists spread out across the southern, and more hospitable continent. Disaster struck in the form of a rain of mycorrhizoid organisms which voraciously attacked all but stone, metal or water. Fire, too, would destroy the menace of "Thread," as the settlers called the devastating showers.

Using their old-world ingenuity, the settlers bio-genetically altered an indigenous life form which resembled the "dragons" of legend. Partnered with a human at birth, these creatures grew to a great size and had abilities desperately needed to combat Thread. Able to chew and digest a phosphine-bearing rock, the dragons could sear the airborne Thread with their fiery breath. The dragons were not only telepathic but telekinetic, thus able to avoid injury during their battles with Thread.

Being a dragon rider required special talents in humans and complete dedication. Thus the dragonriders became a group—apart from those who held the land against the depredations of Thread or those whose craft skills produced other necessities of life in their crafthalls. Over the centuries, the settlers forgot their origins in their struggle to survive against Thread which fell across the land whenever the Red Star's eccentric orbit coincided with Pern's.

There were long intervals, too, when no Thread ravaged the land, when the dragonriders in their Weyrs kept faith with their mighty friends until they would be needed once more to protect the people they were pledged to serve.

During one long interval, twenty-five hundred years after the first landing, very few believed that Thread would return again. Among those few were F'lar, rider of bronze Mnementh, his brother F'nor, brown Canth's rider, and Lessa, diminutive and fiery Weyrwoman, Ramoth's rider, the leaders of Benden Weyr, Pern's last stronghold of dragons and riders. But F'lar, Lessa and F'nor found unexpected support from Masterharper Robinton and Mastersmith Fandarel whose opinions carried weight across Pern.

When Thread once more began its terrible, destructive rain, Benden Weyr rose to meet the ancient challenge. The Lord Holders had no option but to support Pern's one Weyr and struggle to survive against the menace they had thought could no longer threaten them.

Meet Robin Wood's *People of Pern*!

ENTER ROBIN, STAGE LEFT, QUIETLY

The People of Pern has quite truthfully been years in the making—the last year of which was frantic, frenetic, finicking-detail forty-hour stints by Robin Wood to produce the people, and their lifestyle. No easy feat. Who started that crazy notion that artists and writers have an easy life?

It all started with Robin Wood being commissioned in 1982-83 by Mayfair Games to do portraits for major cards in Mayfair's board game of the *Dragonriders of Pern*. I sent her what descriptions I had in the books, as well as more detailed thoughts on the appearances of Lord Holders, Mastercraftsmen, Weyrleaders, and Weyrwomen. Letters flew back and forth; hectic phone calls were exchanged: as she was on a very tight schedule to meet the Mayfair deadline. I suggested well-known faces from which she might model various characters, including the fact that Pern had been a melting pot of all extant Terran ethnic groups. She did an incredibly fine job, showing distinctive personalities in her miniatures: F'lar, Oldive, and the Masterharper still grace my bedroom wall.

(One astonishing incident occurred, right here in Ireland; the manager of the local supermarket bore an incredible resemblance to her portrait of F'lar!)

However, the inception of a real honest-to-woodness portrait book (as near as my memory recalls) occurred at the first Pern-oriented convention, ISTACON, chaired by Angela and Richard Howell in Atlanta, Georgia in 1984. Needless to say, there were many paintings, illustrations and sculp-

ture exhibited in a very good art show which were devoted to the ineffable Dragons of Pern. It is a severe disadvantage for me that conveying artwork on transatlantic flights often results in serious damage to said artwork, and excise tax on importation.

But at the gracious and relaxed ISTACON, there was Robin, wandering about, pencil case on her belt, and watching Kelly Freas do his portrait of me (a stunning birthday present from ISTACON) and chatting up my daughter, Georgeanne Johnson—the model for Moreta—as well as my inestimable attorney, Jay A. Katz. I remember us all talking about doing portraits of the major characters of Pern, as not all people's favorites, like Menolly, Jaxom, Mirrim and Piemur, had been included in the Mayfair Board Game.

Desultory conversations sparkled across transatlantic wastes, or Robin and I would dash into corners at conventions I attended in the States, all through a long period when Robin was unable to get an answer to her initial proposal about a Pern Portrait Gallery. I sent letters, confirming that we had an agreement, and she was duly licensed to create Pern People Portraits. Bless her, she plowed on with the project. Then, in 1986, while I was attending Darkover in Wilmington, Delaware, I got half-kidnapped to the Art Show "where something might interest me." (Hehehe!)

I couldn't have missed it on a moonless night without my glasses. Where absolutely no one attending the Art Show could possibly miss him, there was the Masterharper of Pern, glass of Benden wine raised in a cocky toast, Zair peeping through his silvered hair, superbly limned by Robin Wood's sensitive craftswomanship.

"Did I mind?" she asked me timidly.

"Hell no!" and I put down my name and a fat price. (The portrait did go to Auction, with the provision that I would top all other bids—well, I hesitated just long enough to scare someone half to death.)

Masterharper Robinton occupies pride of place over my mantelpiece and, I must say, I often return his toast of a winter's evening. (I hate to remove him even long enough to restore the dinge in the frame which occurred in carrying him back to Ireland.)

However, it was now plain as the eyes in a dragon's head that we should pursue the notion of a Pern portrait book by Robin. She kept trying to get a contract, but there was no response for an unconscionable length of time. Through the good offices of Bill Fawcett, and with a change of editor, the Donning company approved a contract with Robin—and me—for a *People of Pern* illustration book.

Robin sent me an extremely ambitious list of portraits to be done in full color and several groupings and sketches to be done in prismacolor. Wow! Again I sent her lists of who looked like whom that she could find photos of and suggested my son, Todd Johnson, daughter Georgeanne and Derval Diamond as models for Jaxom, Moreta and Menolly, as they had been the people I visualized when I wrote these characters.

In October 1987, Robin and I had a long session of show and tell at Niagara Falls' CONTRADICTION. Lessa's face was of much concern to me but with me on that trip was an Irish friend who had known the "original" Lessa (Jan Regan) and together we corrected Robin's patient redrafts until we had the Lessa we remembered. We had long discussions on who would have what in their background, and exactly which of the many supporting characters should be included. (In September '87, following CONSPIRACY in Brighton, I had also had my brains picked clean by Jody-Lynn Nye, Bill Fawcett and Todd Hamilton

for their *Guidebook to Pern*, so a lot of corroborative material was readily available to relate to Robin—like did they have cane chairs? Was straw used on floors? Were medical diagrams available? Was cotton used as a fabric fiber? Robin was able to confirm details with Jody-Lynn and Bill but the portraits were major undertakings. And sometime along then, though I had finished the manuscript for *Dragonsdawn*, it was decided not to include those characters as there simply would not be enough time for Robin to do her best on them.

Sketches went back and forth between Robin's home in Cranbury and mine in Greystones. I came to Louisville in March '87 for DRACONIS and Robin had a superb painting of Menolly finished, and more work done on others. We stole time for more discussions on people—she had Todd there for Jaxom, and Gigi for Moreta—and photos were taken of us in our positions on the cover of the book.

Photos of finished work got lost in the shuffle of misguided couriers but, nevertheless, more deadlines were met as Robin exhibited finished work at various East Coast conventions. I had to wait to finish my prose sketches until I had more-or-less finished artwork in hand—as much to comment on Robin's immense attention to background details, definitely one of the subtle strengths of her work in the field, as to remember who I said each character looked like.

We switched faces of two in a phone discussion in early June—guess which! And Robin, fighting a June 30 deadline at Donning, faxed me the last few sketches.

She told me once that it took her 40 hours' work to finish a color portrait. I suspect those forty hours might have been taken in two long gulps at times, with minor breaks for immaterial things like eating or sleeping a bit, or waving cramped hands and dancing up and down on blood-filled legs.

If I were putting in background detail of a portrait of Robin Wood, I would include piles of show biz magazines, arcane woodcuts, heraldry theses (with diagrams), wrinkled tubes of acrylic paints, pencil stubs, soiled paint rags, empty cans of fixative, crumpled sheets of grey sketch paper and pads of sketches of dragons, photographs of many hands, noses, cheeks, heads, portions of anatomy pinned up and down walls, and microwave containers, empty bottles of coke or abandoned cups of coffee/tea. In the foreground, collapsed wearily across an accessory-strewn table, is a figure, probably dressed in fatigue-type overalls (blue to go with her bluey-green eyes), a shaggy head of mid-blonde hair obscuring a pleasant, sleeping face, now wreathed with a well-earned smile of accomplishment, a brow lightly furrowed with resolve NEVER TO GET INTO THIS SORT OF GRIND AGAIN! Paint-stained hands lightly clasp a sturdy bundle, wrapped and taped for mailing, with the address The Donning Company/Publishers plainly visible in Robin's inimitable printing.

If you like *The People of Pern*, maybe if we ask sweetly enough, she might consider doing the people in *Dragonsdawn, Renegades of Pern*, and *All the Weyrs of Pern*. That is, if she hasn't recovered her right mind by then! This woman paints real good. The Dragonlady says so.

ROBIN'S BIT

I first found Pern when I was in high school in Michigan. A friend of mine named Maureen Robertson loaned me *Dragonflight* and *Dragonquest*, which were just out. (I know, that dates me.) She thought I might like them. Like them!

Like most other young artists-to-be I spent a great deal of time in my classes drawing pictures in the margins of my paper when I should have been taking notes. I, of course, started to draw pictures of the People of Pern and their dragons. At one point, I remember, I was caught in this pursuit, and publicly upbraided. I was told I would never need to be able to draw people from Pern, but I would need to know the principal imports and exports of Nicaragua. I feel extremely vindicated!

After this auspicious beginning, I rested my Pern career, and went on to college and Star Trek. Then in 1972 I went to my first science fiction convention, and learned that other people could eat there by selling bad pencil drawings of Mr. Spock. I said to myself, "Self, *I* could do bad pencil drawings of Mr. Spock!" And so I did.

Eventually, the drawings got much better, and the subject material expanded, until Bill Fawcett saw my work at a convention, and approached me about working for Mayfair on their game *The Dragonriders of Pern*. Needless to say, I jumped at the chance. The rest is told in Anne's part of this story.

I will only add that after Anne bid on Masterharper Robinton at that Darkover in 1986, dozens of people came to me to buy prints of the painting, which I was selling at our table in the Huckster's Room. (For those not familiar with cons, that is where people known as Filthy Hucksters set up tables and sell everything from first edition pulps to archaic weapons, passing through jewelry, prints, new and used books, and tapes of filk-songs on the way.)

Someone who came to buy a print asked when I was going to come out with a book showing everyone from the planet of Pern. I replied that I couldn't possibly do that, as color separations cost the earth. But I did mention it to Anne, who responded, "So, when are you?" And when I repeated that I couldn't possibly afford it, she said, "I'll write character sketches. Someone will buy it!" And she was right!! Donning wanted it. *Selling* it, of course, had never occurred to me. I am somewhat slow sometimes. So thank you, whoever you are. Sorry that I don't remember. I was in a bit of shock at the time.

So I started work on the book. Donning had said in the contract how many pictures were to be included. I made a list, contacted Anne, got her OK, and started dressing my friends up and making them stand in funny positions in back of the apartments. (Now lean on your elbow, as if there was a table there.) I took pictures. Other tenants stood around to watch and ask questions. ("What are you doing?" "Ever heard of Anne McCaffrey?" "Like *The Dragonriders of Pern*? Yeah!" "Well, I'm working on a book with her, and he is posing for F'lar." "Oh, *sure*!!!")

Working with Anne on this book was great. All of the portraits are really her images of the people, not just mine. Some of them, like Lessa, had to go through several sketches and police-drawing sessions at the conventions. (Make her chin a bit more pointed, that's good...now her eyebrows should be heavier, no, a little more than that, that's it....) Others I "saw" right from the beginning. And through it all, she was as kind and patient as she could be.

I had Robinton and Menolly done. It was taking too long. So in January, I built a rack in my bathroom that would hold ten paintings at a time, and settled in to do them in batches.

I work by transferring the sketch to a gessoed

masonite board by projecting a slide of it. Then I do an oil underpainting using mostly sepia tones for the skin and things that will be brown, and grey for the rest. This takes several days, as I let one part dry before I paint any adjacent areas. After the whole thing is dry, I apply transparent layers of oil color, so that you can see the underpainting through them. I build them up gradually, often using ten or twelve layers of color. When *that* is dry, I cover the painting with frisket film to protect it, and paint the background. That can take a number of layers, too, although I will admit that I used acrylic paint on some of the backgrounds, to speed things up a bit. Then I touch up the figure, adding more reflected color from the background with more oil glazes, and sign it somewhere. (Many of my friends like to play "find the signature" with my work.)

As it usually has to dry overnight between each layer of paint, all this takes a while. And that is why I had to work on ten or so at a time.

But they are finally finished. Hurrah! And Anne is exactly right about my state when that bright day dawned. You'll have to ask *real* sweetly. (I am very fond of chocolate.) And buy lots of copies of this book. But I did enjoy this, mostly, and if you give me enough time to forget how *hard* it was....

HOLDS OF PERN

The "hold" actually was formed prior to the weyr: being the place of residence, and safety, for the generally agricultural population of Pern.

The first great Hold, Fort (so designated because of its impregnability), was literally carved into a steep precipice where a large cave system of many levels existed, complete with deep reservoirs of water. The main entrance was modified and improved by the skills and tools of the first settlers; the interior caverns were altered and designed according to purpose and need to house nearly 3,000 people.

Since the early volcanic era of Pern developed many such natural shelters on the northern continent, these were utilized by the colonists as the one sure protection from the depredations of Thread. Functional on the outside, the interiors of most Holds, even the smallest, were vivid with color, decoration, paintings, and wall hangings.

Although, in some areas, stone dwellings were constructed where no natural caves existed, a cave provided psychological reassurance, especially against Thread.

A holder, major or minor, was obliged to protect those "beholden" to him during a Pass, supplying them with advice, shelter, and provisions during the 50-Turns. A holder was also responsible for providing assistance to the Weyr which protected him and his from Threadfall—assistance in terms of manpower to destroy any Thread which reached the surface, a tithe to support the Weyr, respect for Dragonrider traditions, and the license to "Search" for suitable Candidates for dragonkind.

Alemi

The third eldest of Menolly's many brothers and sisters, Alemi is most like Menolly in looks and coloring. He is tall and muscular, with weatherbeaten skin and a ready smile. He is the most sympathetic to his talented sister and tries to shield her from their parents' didactic outlook. Alone among her siblings, he appreciates her worth and is proud of her music. But against the unyielding attitude of his Lord Holder, he can do little.

He's an instinctively deft seaman, more flexible than even his father. Most of the crews prefer his ship. Alemi would like to have a small fisher Hold of his own to try some of the ideas he's hatched on long night watches.

The arrival of Elgion, the Harper, puts heart into Alemi, for he finds a true companion and begins to think that maybe his dream might come true.

Alemi is shown casting a net he has woven himself. His straw hat protects him from the burning sun, and the patterned vest identifies him as a Half Circle Seaholder.

ALEMI

© Robin Wood 1988

Elgion

Journeyman Harper Elgion was aghast to discover he was being sent to Half Circle Sea Hold, but he was also complimented by the responsibility of replacing Petiron, the Master Harper's own father, and reviving learning in the desolate Hold.

By nature a volatile man, with an often-whimsical sense of humor, Elgion finds the dour surroundings depressing, but rises firmly above them. Indeed, he reaps quite a harvest of goodwill from people starved for wit and music.

Although he does not complete an unwritten request to find Petiron's talented apprentice, he does find an unexpected companion in Alemi and settles down well in his first assignment.

ELGION

© Robin Wood 1988

Yanus and *Mavi*

The most positive thing to be said about this pair is that they mean well. They contrive and thrive in a dangerous occupation that leaves little scope for the mistakes to which man, and woman, are heir. In fact, they do not understand "mistake," since they clearly know that one does one's duty by Hold and Weyr and a good meal and a secure place to rest should follow such adherence. They believe in hard work for idle hands, making do or doing without, and in no quarter given or taken. They have neither humor nor insight, and how they produced a musically talented, sensitive personality like Menolly would have mystified them if they had had an ounce of curiosity in their make-up. But they mean well and do their duty.

MAVI

& YANUS

©Robin Wood 1988

Petiron

With a personality as complex as his son's, Petiron left the Harper Hall when his son was nominated Masterharper so as to leave Robinton free to make decisions. Petiron was also brokenhearted by the death of his beloved wife and immuring himself in the eastern fens at least took him far from any chance of stray memories of her.

Quite as brilliant a musician as his son, adept on every instrument, his duties at Half Circle Sea Hold allowed him not only time to play long hours but entranced audiences on long winter and stormy nights. The children he taught were hungry for knowledge, and when joint-ail made it hard for him to finger any of his beloved instruments, he had Menolly to teach and play for him. In her, and in his son, he instilled the love of music in all its forms, and encouraged another genuine talent.

A tall man, gaunt and gnarled with age, his expression rarely revealed inner turmoil or anger and his eyes, brilliant but of no particular shade for any length of time, remained sharp until they closed in death.

PETIRON

©Robin Wood 1988

21

Jaxom

Son of the Usurper Fax and his unwilling wife, Lady Gemma, Jaxom was born after his father's death and is very lucky to be alive. Happily, he is a fortunate physical blend of his parents. His facial features resemble those of Lady Gemma, who can trace a strong connection to Ruathan blood. Taller than his father, and of strong physique, he has black hair which he wears long and back from his face. His eyes are grey-green and deep-set below arched brows.

Reared by the loyal but tormented Lytol, and firmly educated to accede to a high position, Jaxom's fine intelligence has been honed, and a sense of duty and responsibility indelibly instilled in heart and mind. He is sensitive, thoughtful, and so impartial that he is his own worst advocate. He will be a power in the Turns of this Fall, living well into the Interval. More so than any of his contemporaries, he is a far-seeing tactician, with the needs of Hold, Weyr, and Hall his firm priority.

Thanks to his inadvertent Impression of the white dragon, Ruth, and to his innate sense of justice, he will become the obvious arbitrator as Fall ends. Jaxom has been trained to carry out his purpose as no other on the planet. His pose here, with distance viewer in hand, is appropriately against the spring-flowered valley near the Ice Lake above Ruatha Hold.

23

Lytol

Some people are born unlucky. Lytol has suffered, and survived, almost every evil that can befall a man on Pern. For most of his contemporaries, to be born in the Weyr and Impress a dragon would have been considered the best of good luck. But Lytol's brown dragon, Larth, was fatally injured in the Spring Games and Lytol did not die.

Leaving the Weyr brought a second trauma. Then, when he tenaciously began a new craft, Lytol succeeded well enough to become a master, marry a kind woman, and father daughters. His craft took him to High Reaches Hold just about the time Fax usurped it. His daughters and wife were pretty and were coveted by Fax. Two of his girls managed to escape. The other committed suicide and her mother died of a heart seizure. Once again Lytol was left with nothing.

Only a man of exceptional character and stability could have endured such personal catastrophes, so he seemed the logical person—to F'lar—to foster a newborn, orphaned baby who would grow to Hold Ruatha. Undemonstrative Lytol could never display to his charge, Jaxom, how much the boy meant to him—a grip on reality, a bulwark against utter spiritual defeat, and a triumph over misfortune of a tremendous scale.

Lytol's unending battle with tragedy is engraved on his features, in his greying hair and sad brown eyes, but his integrity and strength of will are also visible and he is considered wise and just as well as extremely capable. And Jaxom loves him deeply.

25

Deelan and Dorse

Deelan is the motherly sort, fussy, plump, and good-natured, but not overly blessed with intelligence. She has common sense regarding everyday matters but does not look much beyond the present. She is sincerely devoted to her milkson and thus also fosters her own son's dislike of Jaxom. This manifested itself in petty outbursts and wrangles when the boys were younger, and often subtle subversions as they became older and Dorse realized the gap between their stations and abilities.

Perversely, Dorse admires his foster brother as well as envying him. When push comes to shove, Dorse is stoutly behind Jaxom.

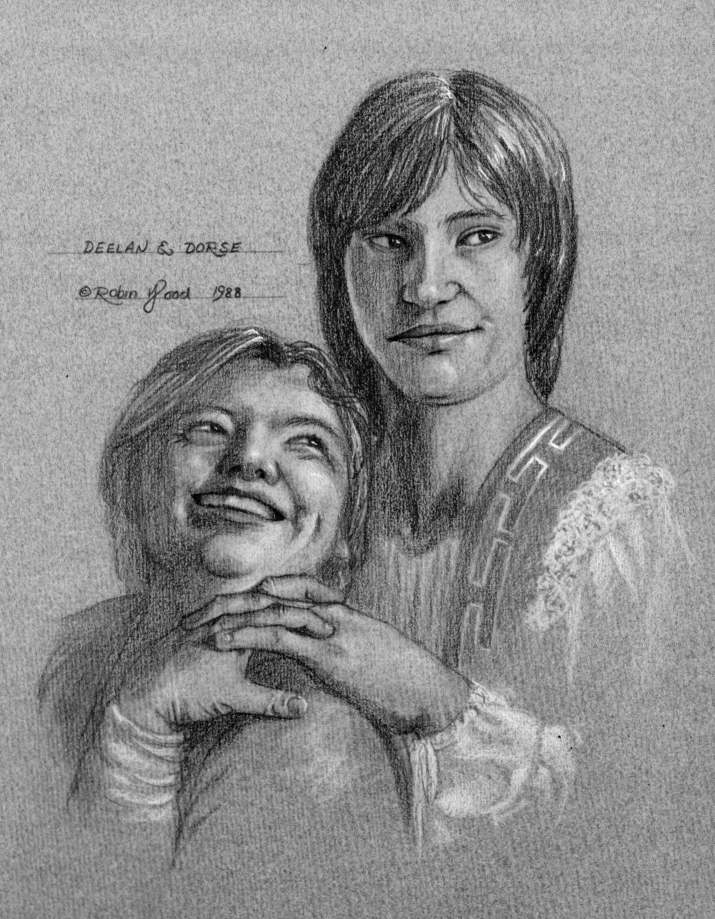

DEELAN & DORSE

©Robin Wood 1988

Brand

Brand is an able second to Lyton's wardenship and is as interested in Jaxom retaining his future as Lord Holder of Pern as F'lar and Lessa. A good administrator, Brand enjoys the challenge of rebuilding Ruatha to its former prominence. He has a steady eye, a steady hand, a firm mouth, and considerably more humor in him than the dour Lytol. Jaxom finds him more approachable and trusts him implicitly. He is certainly sympathetic to the young Lord and discreetly assists him when he can.

He is not a demonstrative man, either, but Brand relaxes considerably when he Impresses a blue fire-lizard and becomes more open and flexible.

BRAND

©Robin Wood 1988

29

Corana

Corana is a pretty girl, sister to Fidello, a small holder. Well aware that a Lord Holder should be obeyed. Corana is quite willing to dally with Jaxom. Because he is a gentle and personable young man, she shyly encourages his attentions. A more sophisticated young woman might have put off Jaxom's tentative approach, so Corana's undemanding and uninhibited response was exactly right for him.

CORANA

© Robin Wood 1988

Fax and Lady Gemma

A hard, implacable, ruthless man, Fax is nevertheless not unattractive. He is heavy-set and of medium height. It is his cold expression and almost colorless eyes which add to his formidableness. He wears his hair cut close to his scalp for, in his bid to extend his control over seven Holds in the West, he is often in battle gear. More greedy for power than material gain, his tactics are brutal and heartlessly enforced. We may witness his cruelty to Lady Gemma and his seduction of any attractive women who comes his way.

He controls his minions with an iron grasp of their foibles and entertains no doubts of his invincibility—his fatal error. Had he not been cut down by F'lar, he would most certainly have tyrannized the entire West before gathering his forces to invade the lush plains of Telgar.

Gemma, a woman of great pride and courage, is prematurely aged by her miserable life with the self-styled Lord Fax. Kept pregnant by Fax as an unremarkable way to end their formal alliance, she manages to retain her dignity and humanity, but she has been left with absolutely no illusions. We can but honor her fortitude.

FAY

& GEMMA

©Robin Wood 1988

Sharra

Not pretty, certainly not in Corana's fashion, Sharra has irregular features, a nose almost too long for her face and a chin too firm for beauty. Her mid-dark hair is sun bleached and her eyes are a hazel that alter between green and gold. Her skin is tanned year round. She is tall, athletic, and a very independent person, able to enjoy her own company for long periods. She is frequently in contention with her domineering older brother, Toric, self-styled Lord Holder of all southern Pern. She has become fascinated by the herbs and plants of the Southern Continent and spends much time searching them out to replenish her stores. She wants to learn more about the healing craft but, since her skills are instinctive, she will need little more formal training. It is no wonder that the artist has posed her with a full basket of medicinal flowers, the lush tropical foliage framing her, her thick hair twined with blossoms.

With her fine sense of integrity, volatile good nature, and independent attitude, she is a perfect match for Jaxom, supporting and encouraging him, and striding next to him in all his endeavors.

Toric

A big man physically, unusually tall with a square, powerful frame, sun-bleached hair, cold grey eyes and an uncertain temperament, Toric in many ways emulates Fax's aggrandisement. And the Southern Continent is ripe for exploitation. However, Toric is no fool. He is a born organizer and a good administrator though he is quick enough to punish the inept or inert.

Shrewdly he manipulates Oldtimers and northern Holders to assist his own plans of control and domination. Needing loyal supporters and industrious settlers for his projects, he makes a careful selection of disgruntled renegades and offers them land of his Holding in the fruitful South with its semi-tropical climate and "easy living." But he holds all supplies and controls all the shipping to and from the other continent. A clever but cautious man, he feels secure and quite willing to flaunt the aid of the Dragonriders since Southern takes no real harm from Threadfall.

Few make the mistake of underestimating Toric.

Lord Groghe

Fort was the first Hold and consequently its Lord Holder often considers himself the first Lord Holder, to whom all others must defer. Whether from tradition or the worth of the individual, the Lord Holder maintains considerable control over the decisions and opinions of the entire Northern Continent.

Fortunately, Lord Groghe is a capable man, tall, imposing, with a broad torso, thick thighs, and bulging calves. He has a florid complexion, a booming voice, and a tendency to treat women as slightly imperfect creatures lacking in wit. Nevertheless, he is a fair man, and rules a large family and many dependents with a firm hand. Rather skeptical at first about the return of Thread, once convinced, he throws his weight behind the Dragonriders with no hesitation. Lord Groghe's abilities were fortunately what stopped Fax on the very borders of Fort.

GROGHE

©Robin Wood 1988

CRAFTHALLS

Based on a structure of apprentice/master, all the necessary skills to keep the population of Pern supplied with anything from rare wooden barrels to fishhooks, fine wool to leather for boots, and specially adapted breeding stock were represented by Craft Halls. These Halls also trained young people, instruction generally commencing when the aspiring apprentice turned twelve. The usual length of tuition was five years, though in some crafts, like Smithcraft or Healers, it took up to ten years for a person to gain a journeyman's rank, and additional study was required to attain Mastery.

Masters could specialize in various facets of their particular Craft and teach apprentices the particular craft secrets, jealously (sometimes too zealously) guarded.

Each Craft chose an administrative or executive Master, generally then styled Mastersmith, or Masterharper, who governed, with a suitable quorum of other Masters, the entire Craft. Journeymen were assigned to holds, weyrs, or other halls as requests came to the Mastercraft Hall involved. Every major hold boasted halls of many crafts, for convenience and prestige.

Craft Halls were autonomous so that their produce could not be monopolized by a greedy Lord Holder. Craft items, and raw materials, were freely bartered and distributed across the northern continent, generally at local Gathers. Some Crafts sent journeymen throughout the land at special times to obtain special commissions. A craft could call an embargo on a holder for abuse of Hall. Most crafts would support their fellows in such a matter, so incidents of embargo were rare.

Menolly

A tall, gawky girl, slightly knock-kneed and bony, with a long, thin face and a pronounced nose, the second thing one notices about Menolly is a mop of dark, curling hair which partially hides her face. She hates to cut her hair. She has long, graceful, extremely strong fingers in a narrow but competent hand. Her sudden smiles light up her face and give her an inner radiance that astonishes those she rewards with her happiness.

Totally unaware of her physical self, Menolly lives for music, any sort of music. Sensitive, compassionate, perceptive, and capable of intense concentration, she was exactly the temperament and personality to learn all that Harper Petiron had to teach her.

Because music comes so easily to her, she is unaware of what a tremendous gift, and ability, she possesses—a modesty which does her almost more harm than good. Loyal to a fault, she gives her heart unconditionally to the Masterharper and, later, to Sebell, but they are both musicians enough to never take advantage of her and to encourage her in her work.

Oldive

How to describe a man who exudes confidence and compassion? Oldive has a fey sense of humor, given to grimaces which contort a great, lean face, impenetrable dark eyes which keep their own counsel, and thick eyebrows. He also has a twisted spine which compresses his upper torso down to his pelvis so that he constantly regards people from a slanted position.

He is a consummate healer, with ready information on all sorts of odd ailments and their cure. He can effect the most dramatic recoveries for the ailing and set bones to heal straight and sound no matter how badly broken. He is much in demand but very often sends someone in his place no matter who calls for his services because he cannot travel easily. If a dragon comes for him, he is more likely to undertake a journey.

Behind him are some of the many charts which line the walls of his quarters, some of them quite faded. He is scrupulous in grinding and preparing his own powders and potions.

Piemur

Young and of slight stature when he first meets Menolly, he becomes her first and firmest friend in the Harper Hall. Clever, ingenious, intelligent, and devious, Piemur is a self-serving scamp of the first order but of a generous nature. Fascinated by the fire-lizards, he inveigles himself into Menolly's good graces to have a closer look at them and becomes enamoured of Menolly as well, quite willing to instruct her in the mysteries of her new home.

Piemur is also, though he might not admit it, a brave and courageous person and, once his beautiful treble voice changes, flexible enough to seek a new career. It is as much a surprise to him as to others that he decides to remain in Southern and explore its mysterious challenge. He turns into quite an explorer with Farli, his golden fire-lizard and Stupid, his orphan runner beast.

Robinton, The Masterharper of Pern

Of all the characters of Pern, Robinton is the first of two modeled on real living personages—the second is Menolly, oddly enough. But Master Robinton, who came on as a spear carrier in *Dragonflight*, develops into the Pernese equivalent of a Macchiavelli—a finger in every pot and an ear in every hall and craft—thanks to a network of loyal Harpers throughout Pern. He does, however, have the best interests of his world firmly in his mind and heart.

Tall, gaunt, with a lined, saturnine face, Robinton's generous smile hides personal tragedies. His alliance with Silvina, Headwoman of the Harper Hall, resulted in Camo, a mentally retarded, gentle giant, and Robinton contrives not to father a second child. He is the Spokesperson for Pern at large, confidante of Lords, Masters, and Weyrleaders with a vast store of sensible advice and counsel. He has no conception of how deeply he is revered through the world or how much he means to people individually. He is Court Jester, Balladeer, and Master Arbiter without admitting to himself that he is all these personas and more.

He adores Lessa—which everyone realizes though he never admits it—and Benden wine, which he imbibes all too deeply and frequently. He is, fortunately, possessed of an incredible tolerance for alcohol and never appears the worse for wear. Indefatigable, he has probably travelled more distance than anyone else in the world, and becomes quite testy when his health requires him to settle in Cove Hold. But then, the rest of the world comes to him. As well it should!

Sebell

The Masterharper's own acknowledged choice of successor, Sebell goes about discreetly improving his own understanding of the responsibilities which will one day fall on his shoulders. He is so discreet that people are sometimes unaware of his presence until he speaks out—which he will if he feels he ought. A sterling young man who bides his time, as well as his counsel, he is slightly taller than Master Robinton, though he tends to slump to hide the extra height. He has dark hair over a high forehead and an intelligent brow. He has a "good" face, showing his strong character and purpose but it is his quiet strength that will suddenly impress an audience as well as the rare quality of patient forebearance with the follies of the world. He reveres the Masterharper and adores Menolly but bides his time in all things.

Sebell is portrayed in a rare moment of relaxation, seated on one of the deep window ledges of the upper story of the Harper Hall, playing the harp, his favorite instrument. His guitar, drum, and tabourine are within each as well as the heavy leather pouch which carries his travel necessities.

51

Silvina

A gracious, energetic, and capable woman, Silvina is also a lovely one with dark hair, very white skin, and luminous eyes set in a broad-cheeked face. She smiles readily but is equally quick to frown if needed, for she has many people to manage and many tasks to do. She speaks her mind and no one is left in doubt as to where they stand in her graces.

If she regrets that her liaison with the Masterharper was shortlived and Camo the result, she never mentions it but scolds Robinton impartially with all the other people she mothers. Tenacious in her loyalties, she yet has too much common sense to permit emotion to interfere with rational decisions.

Silvina poses before one of the highly decorated panels of her small office in the Harper Hall, displaying the keys of spice cabinets behind her.

Brudegan

Journeyman Brudegan is the much-aggrieved choral instructor, struggling to get young men to sing on pitch, in tempo, and with good enunciation. "E-NUN-ciate!" is his oft-repeated phrase. He is never quite satisfied with the results, superb as they often are. He is a dark-haired man in his mid-thirties, not at all athletic in appearance, though he carries himself well, as a trained singer must. He has broad cheekbones, a round face, and the jowls of a tenor. Brudegan is rarely seen outside the chorus room, and then humming a phrase from the tenor part of the latest score.

BRUDEGAN

© Robin Wood 1986

Talmor

Talmor is tall, with an appealingly bony face and an inquisitive, almost wistful expression. He wears his thin, dark hair back, swept off his high forehead. His humor can occasionally lead him into trouble.

Talmor is a good teacher, with the patience necessary to instill lessons and command discipline, but he really enjoys the challenge of playing Master Domick's music and the stimulation of group playing. He's a baritone, with a powerful voice and such a mobile face that he often ends up playing villains.

TALMOR

©Robin Wood 1988

Brolly and *Ranly*

They are particular cronies of the mischievous Piemur, whom they imitate and follow because he is far more adventurous—and devious—than they could ever be.

Ranly is the elder, but not necessarily the wiser, and sometimes acts more self-assured than he actually is. They are both loyal friends to Piemur and, by association, to Menolly, who has awed the entire apprentice population by owning nine fire-lizards. Ranly sings alto, while Brolly has a good treble (though not as good as Piemur's). They both end up as instrument makers, continuing under Master Jerint's aegis as journeymen.

BROLLY

& RANLY

© Robin Wood 1988

Dunca

A short, dumpy woman, Dunca has bright black restless eyes that find shortcomings in anything she does not herself do. Her cheeks are often puffed out with indignation, if not outrage, at some minor infraction. With no imagination, she imagines many slights and dangers, and is a "poison neat" holder. But she is just the sort of officious person to oversee young, well-bred women.

Hypocritical and always hoping that a pleased parent will slip her the odd mark or two for her chaperonage, she makes pets of the girls with the more prestigious parents, to the disadvantage of those more worthy of consideration.

DUNCA

©Robin Wood 1988

Amania

Daughter to a craftsmaster, Amania is also in the Harper Hall to meet a suitable husband. She is a handsome girl and more intelligent than either Pona or Briala. But she is content to take the back seat since that is an easier way to get by at Dunca's.

AMANIA

© Robin Wood 1988

Audiva

A Craftsmaster's daughter, Audiva is the most outgoing of the collection living at Dunca's. She has a quick smile, a pretty face, and enough moral courage to stand up to Pona when a stand becomes necessary. She also wants to learn more than the other girls and becomes Menolly's first real girl friend. She has courage enough to take Menolly's side in a crunch.

AUDIVA

© Robin Wood 1988

Briala

A pretty child, vain about her hair, which she is constantly rearranging, Briala is easily led by Pona, who has the more aggressive personality. With a different leader, she would be a nicer person. She is in Harper Hall only because her ambitious parents hope that her prettiness will attract a good alliance with one of the fosterlings at Fort Hold.

BRIALA

©Robin Wood 1988

Pona

One of the girls who go to the Harper Hall to improve their musical abilities, Pona takes great pride in her position as ranking "girl," for her grandfather is Lord Holder of Boll. She does not wear her rank well, using it unfairly as a weapon. Dunca, who is easily impressed, upholds her in this. A short-ish, plump child, without much character in her face, or elegance in her appearance, she is basically a bully, so sets the attitudes of most of the other girls in Dunca's cottage.

PONA

© Robin Wood 1988

Camo, Abuna and Kayla

Camo is the son of Silvina and Masterharper Robinton, a large and amiable man who is lucky to have survived a difficult birth. He is fascinated by Menolly's fire-lizards and spends hours watching the creatures. However, he has duties in the Harper Hall and, with patient reminders, he is useful and protected.

Abuna and Kayla are sisters who manage the kitchen at Harper Hall, supervised by Silvina and, generally, assisted by Camo and any number of apprentices who might be on a punishment detail. They bicker constantly about minor tasks, with no real ill-feeling but a certain competitiveness which generally makes the work go more easily. They are both married to journeymen serving Master Arnor. They are devoted to Masterharper Robinton and the Hall and quite happy to take Silvina's orders even though they might, from time to time, contest them.

CAMO, ABUNA
& KAYLA
©Robin Wood 1988

71

Master Arnor

A perfectionist, as all Masters must be, Arnor is as dry as some of the records he keeps in his tiny, precise handwriting ("More lines to the page.").

His shoulders are stooped, his thin chest concave from bending over manuscripts, and his index finger is ridged from hours of holding a pen. He has a pasty complexion, a high forehead, and a perpetual squint and frown.

Advanced joint-ail does not help his temper, but he persists, despite the discomfort, in copying "important" documents. He trusts few people to transcribe the fading inks which, in truth, he has trouble reading since his eyesight has deteriorated.

He tends to be officious and restricts the use of archival materials in an often erratic fashion. Every Harper Hall apprentice must learn copying and musical annotation from him, but he makes the learning no joy. He and Master Morshal are kindred spirits.

MASTER ARNOR

© Robin Wood 1988

73

Master Domick

A short, stocky man; self-assured, arrogant in his musicality, demanding a high standard of performance from anyone whom he teaches, Master Domick is the resident instrumental composer for the Harper Hall. He delights in intricate musical forms and quite loses himself in playing with others, impatient though he is with their lesser abilities.

After many years of trying to instill the tenets of his craft into dull and unappreciative heads, he relies on sarcasm to sting apprentices into doing their best. He is capable of sly jokes, droll rather than wounding, but he is too intelligent to be narrow-minded and deplores the attitude of some of his colleagues.

MASTER DOMICK

© Robin Wood 1988

Master Jerint

Supremely happy in his high-ceilinged workshops, surrounded by the tools and raw materials of his trade, Master Jerint is a superb craftsman and one of those rare people who can instill in his sometimes reluctant students the precepts of his skill. He has a droll sense of humor, but is perhaps more flexible in his attitudes than some of the other masters. Despite the discipline he maintains while they are working, he is sympathetic to the outside interests of his boys. He has a variety of ways of handling them so that they never know what Master Jerint will do. He might appear to be absent-minded but, in fact, he rarely misses a thing—including the materials which disappear from his stocks, which the boys surreptitiously sell at the Gathers.

MASTER JERINT

©Robin Wood 1988

Master Morshal

Master Morshal does not see eye to eye at all with a composer. Morshal does not approve of change or alteration and tries to pass on the tradition of Harper Hall excellence as it has been handed down from the beginning of time. He is supercilious, dogmatic, and utterly unimaginative. He is more mathematician than musician, though he'd be horrified if someone told him. He excels in drilling apprentices in the basics of the Craft. He looks for faults whenever he can, being dissatisfied with his present rank in the Harper Hall. His sallow complexion is set off by greying locks, tinged with yellow. He has absolutely no sense of humor, so it is not surprising that he is not popular with the boys in the Harper Hall.

MASTER MORSHAL

© Robin Wood 1988

Master Shonagar

A barrel of a man who affects a variety of poses with great success, Master Shonagar has a heavy hand, many chins, and very bright, all-seeing eyes. As he sits, he seems more chest than arm and leg and he is indolent to the point of immobility. He is scrupulously fair to the boys and accurately judges their abilities in their first sessions with him. He affects to be uninvolved with any of his students but, in fact, he is always hoping to find the one singer who deserves his teaching. Perhaps because most of the adolescent voices he must teach are so shortlived, he must always be disappointed by the ephemeral. Master Shonagar is, however, even more talented at drawing the best out of those he does teach, for he knows more about "voice" than Domick knows about composition. And the apprentices adore him in spite of himself.

MASTER SHONAGAR

© Robin Wood 1988

Fandarel

The Smithcraft master is an immense, burly man. In height and breadth, Fandarel is one of the biggest men on Pern. His face is seamed with coal dust and broken blood vessels from extremes of heat and cold. His hands are scarred from wielding hammers and dealing with molten metals. He tends to start speaking in a booming voice, made harsh from shouting over machinery noises, then recalls the need to modulate and will often whisper, to the dismay of his listeners.

Nothing escapes his curious, oddly mild glance. His goal is the efficient operation of all things: *Waste not, want not.* For all of that, he is a generous, warm-hearted man, a perfectionist, a genius. Fandarel is a man much needed in his time on Pern, and few can have a better accolade than that.

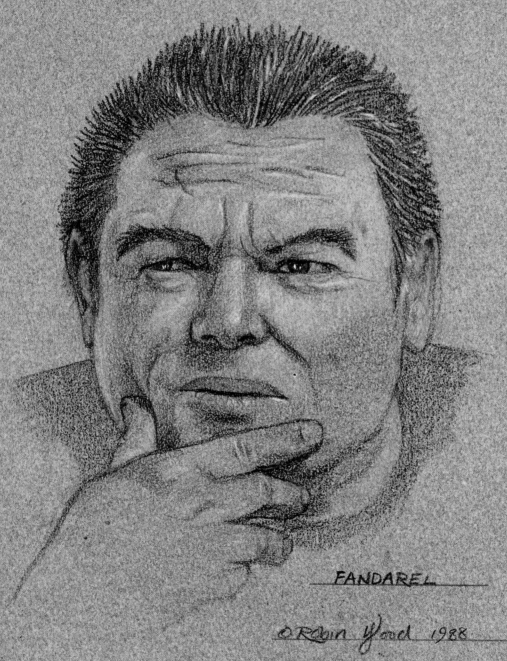

FANDAREL

©Robin Wood 1988

Terry

A Smith Master in his own right, Terry has a genius for organization and management second only to Mastersmith Fandarel's. He is also an innovator, forever fiddling with equipment to improve it to an efficiency expected by Fandarel. Terry augments his own keen mind by constant browsing through moldering Records, hoping to find some ancient mechanicals with modern usage. He has often taken old wisdom and adapted it to Pern's needs with surprisingly "efficient" results.

He is not a very prepossessing man, balding, with a fringe of lank hair, a prominent nose, and a round face, but his piercing dark eyes miss little, even when he appears to be deep in thought. Not a large man, he is, however, exceedingly strong from a lifetime spent at forges and heaving about resisting machineries. He finds the absent-minded Wansor a bit of a trial at times but, on the other hand, he'll turn the Workshop upside down to accommodate Wansor's requirements.

TERRY

©Robin Wood 1988

Wansor

Wansor is a man of medium height with squinting eyes, much in need of the glasses he produces for corrective lenses. He is balding and stoop-shouldered, with a quick, almost nervous smile. He also has a tendency to stammer when he can't get his words out fast enough.

WANSOR

© Robin Wood 1988

WEYRFOLK

Natural geological structures were also utilized for the habitation of the Dragons of Pern and their dedicated riders as well as the weyrfolk who tended both. For weyrs, the craters of extinct volcanoes, riddled with small caverns, proved to be eminently suitable to house the large dragons and their riders. Ideally, there needed to be an eastern facing wall on the crater for the establishment of Star Stones which were placed to determine if the Red Star were close enough to make another Pass over Pern. A lake was required, man-made or natural, in which dragons could bathe, and sufficient space for a paddock where the herd beasts that supplied meat to both dragon and weyrfolk could be maintained.

The Dragonriders of Pern were an elite group, chosen by the dragons with whom they were partnered. During a Pass, when the queen dragons tended to produce larger clutches, Impression might be made with younger boys. During Intervals, when there were fewer matings, older Candidates were presented. Preferably chosen from among the youngsters bred to the Weyr, the Dragonriders could also "Search" for possible dragonmates within hold and hall. It was generally considered an honor to be chosen. Certainly few ever sought to leave the Weyr.

F'lar

F'lar has always felt there is a purpose to his life, and he has honed his strengths and perceptions so that he would be ready to serve and save his planet. He is capable of bursts of intuition that can make the necessary leap from present fact to future extrapolation.

He has absolutely no vanity, which is just as well, for he is the sort of born leader that men follow willingly. Men are infected by his enthusiasm and dedication, and women desire to entice him. He presents a stern appearance, but his frequent smile is devastating. He has a gay and ringing laugh. His unusual amber eyes, inherited from his mother, dominate his strong-featured face. He gets his level, sometimes daunting, expression from his father, as well as his strength of purpose and tall, lean, muscular build.

He and Lessa complement each other in many ways. He is more at ease in company and is able to converse with anyone. He is not as implacable as she is, and can make allowances for people even as he urges them to greater effort. He couldn't care less what he puts on his back—so long as his fighting gear is in good repair—but he humors Lessa, who would rather see him wear garments appropriate to his rank.

F'lar has absolutely no fear (he's always had Mnementh to support and encourage him) and only momentarily did he ever allow his own self-confidence to falter. His belief in his purpose to ready Pern to fight Thread is entrenched in his mind, heart, and soul. With Lessa as his partner, he has the human confidante he needs and cherishes.

91

Lessa

Ah, the woman who started it all, by waking up cold one morning and seeing things in the dawn, and yearning for revenge.

Lessa is not an easy person to get to know—lack of practice on her part—and she holds herself aloof from casual friendships. She takes her responsibilities very seriously, often without a leavening dollop of humor; she's a shade too prosaic most times but occasionally, with F'lar, F'nor, N'ton, and especially Master Robinton, she will relax and enjoy herself without inhibition. And always with Ramoth, who commands more response from her than any human.

Lessa has a quick temper and it flares unexpectedly but, on more sober reflection, she will often realize that she has been wrong—just get her to admit it! Lessa has no time for fools and shirkers and she says what she means.

In form, she is of small stature, almost painfully thin, with fine bones and features. She is obsessively neat, and secretly delights in the fine clothes her position as Weyrwoman now allows her. She is not personally vain because she cannot appreciate the tremendous charisma she exudes. She does, however, take particular pains and care of her heavy, long black hair.

93

F'nor

Much like a blurred, slightly shorter and more awkward version of his older brother, F'nor has an open personality and an approach to life mellowed by his mother, Manora. He is gentler by nature, more thoughtful, and merrier. F'nor is quite willing to follow where F'lar leads, though he's one of the few people on Pern who will contradict F'lar. Impressing Canth came as a distinct surprise to F'nor, who hadn't really thought he'd be good enough to become a dragonrider.

Though far more flexible than F'lar or Lessa, F'nor clearly sees his own duties and discharges his responsibilities faithfully. He knows who he is and is well content to be F'lar's half-brother and wingsecond. He is fiercely loyal to F'lar.

The intensity of his love for and devotion to Brekke astonishes him. He cherishes her even above F'lar, though not quite above Canth. When Brekke starts having their five fine strong sons and two daughters, he is by far the most doting, but firm, father in the Weyr.

Brekke

Gentle, quiet Brekke maintains a serene expression though she is, even after she Impresses Wirenth, terribly unsure of herself. She hides that uncertainty even from her adored queen dragon. She is so self-critical and self-doubting that she just *knows* she is unworthy of Wirenth, and worries constantly that her Hold upbringing will inhibit her marvelous dragon.

She devotes herself to being useful, helpful, kind, thoughtful, and self-effacing as if to repay someone for her amazing luck at having Impressed such a lovely queen as Wirenth. However, Brekke genuinely likes nursing and enjoys all the endless, finicky tasks that go along with it. She has an infinite, selfless capacity for caring, encompassing the worst-behaved of the foster children (like Mirrim) and animals.

The shock and joy of discovering that such a person as F'nor loved her is almost too much for her. The thought of losing him (and Canth) spurs her to a superhuman effort that saves the pair at a critical time.

Discarding the last of her Holdbred restrictions, Brekke provides F'nor with a large family which she manages with ease, love, and a firm discipline that surprises even Lessa.

© Robin Wood 1988

97

F'lessan

F'lessan was born merry, despite the difficulties of his birth, that nearly took his mother's life. He is the only child of Lessa and F'lar, though not F'lar's only child. He has his mother's grey eyes and his father's black hair, and he is more willowy of build than F'lar.

He gives the appearance of gliding through life, being possessed of a most equitable personality, immense good humor, and willingness. Only Jaxom and Sharra ever realize that he can be quite reflective and shrewd. He does not, however, wish to be encumbered by the responsibilities his parents have assumed. He is an excellent dragonrider, well paired with Golanth. He has always been proud that he Impressed a bronze, even if he did nothing else that brought complete approval from his rather daunting parents. The prospect of flying Thread most of his adult years seems like an ideal occupation for someone skilled in his craft and able to meet the challenge.

Above all, he likes the numerous girls that he meets in his position and unabashedly makes use of his fine singing voice and modest ability to play the guitar. He is fond of saying that if he hadn't Impressed Golanth, he'd have made a fine Harper.

Manora

Manora gives the outward expression of calm competence and confident dignity and there isn't anyone in the Weyr who will willingly disobey her. She is tall, womanly, with white hair now. With her clever, shrewd eyes and tremendous energy, she is posed on one of the Weyr's carved stone chairs which gives her a regal appearance quite appropriate to her manner. She sees nothing unusual in being totally occupied and well organized, but she can be kindly ruthless with those who shirk their duties and gentle with the weakminded or infirm. She knows to the featherweight and the potlid what the resources of the Weyr are, and who is best qualified to do which task—and in how much time. Because she is both knowledgeable and persuasive, she gets everything accomplished without resentment. And no one would dare flaunt Manora.

Privately, she disliked R'gul as Weyrleader but then no one, not even his eldest son, F'lar, could match the incomparable F'lon whom she had adored even after he had ended their association. Believing devoutly in F'lon's view of the Weyr's imminent future, she willingly assumed the onerous duties of Headwoman, thus assisting F'lon and later his son, F'lar, by thriftily managing the domestic affairs of the Weyr and subtly encouraging his aims.

A shrewd judge of character, Manora assessed the thin, almost ugly waif whom F'lar found at Ruatha as an indomitable spirit, exactly the sort of person needed for the new queen dragon. In much the same way, Manora saw Kylara as a divisive personality, dangerously self-centered and immature.

Manora, for all her self-effacing, quiet dignity, must always be considered a prime force in the resurgence of the Dragonriders on Pern.

Mirrim

A fosterling, the child of blue rider L'trel and the daughter of a holder who disowned her, Mirrim was ignored by both her indolent mother and her father. An appealing child, desirous only of pleasing, she easily assumed whatever manner would please, following Manora and trying "to help," or Brekke, when she arrived at the Weyr. It was to patient and kind Brekke that Manora and Lessa assigned the difficult child, Mirrim.

She is too quick and willing to find favor with her peers, "showing them up" if they dawdle or skivv off. To win approval from her idols, Mirrim is often far too tactless about these minor transgressions and has earned herself many bruises and much loneliness. She is eager, responsible, certainly too impressionable, and always trying to please Lessa, Manora, Brekke, or whoever. With so many strong, different role models, it is small wonder that Mirrim had an identity crisis, not at all abetted by inadvertently Impressing green Path—shown here still wet from hatching. The astonished radiance of Impression quite transforms Mirrim.

When she relaxes this urge to imitate one or another of the women she admires, the real Mirrim is a loving, sensitive, capable girl. And once she finally accepts who she is, she will find that T'gellan has been patiently waiting for her all this long while.

N'ton

Craftbred from Nabol, a hard hold in which to make any sort of a living, Naton was tremendously excited to be chosen on Search but not very confident of his chances of Impressing, despite the fact that he could understand F'nor's brown Canth from the moment he got to Benden Weyr. When first bronze Lioth, and then brown Tris became his companions, he felt he had come a long way. He was determined to improve enough to be noticed by F'lar. Some of his Nabol-bred caution always kept him from overstepping the bounds of common sense. A natural leader, his wingriders trusted him and he knew to a hair how far he could push them, their dragons, and himself.

He had feared for a while that he might have to pair off with Kylara and Prideth into the newly established Southern Weyr. He didn't like the woman, though she fascinated him, and he was mightily relieved when she appeared to prefer poor T'bor, who idolized her dazzling blonde beauty. Later N'ton wondered if he might not have had more control over Kylara, simply because he wasn't besotted with her, and thus could have helped avoid the deaths of the two queens, Wirenth and Prideth. By then, F'lar and Lessa had honored him by making him Weyrleader of Fort and whipping that discouraged group into shape.

N'ton much preferred fighting to management, but his craft training gave him the background he needed and he would have done anything for the Benden Weyrleaders.

G'dened

G'dened is the son of oldtimers D'ram and Fanna, the Weyr-leaders of Ista Weyr. He was just the right age to be flexible when his parents followed Lessa to the new crisis on Pern. He was reared on stories of the Weyr's valiant history and Pern's struggle, yet he would have just missed being old enough to fight Fall in his own time. Consequently, he is well-primed to be a rider of bronze Baranth, and to succeed his father as Weyrleader.

He also finds young and vibrant heroes to worship in F'lar and Lessa, preferring their company to that of his own because they grumble so much about the changes which occurred in the long Interval. Brown of hair and eye, but with the sallow complexion which reflects the hot Istan sun, his favorite off-duty activity is swimming in the clear waters around the Big Island. Aided by Baranth, who loves water as much as he, they often dive quite deep, picking up unusual stones and objects from the sands. Baranth is not at all averse to floating, wings extended, while G'dened fishes. There are usually a few for him when G'dened is successful.

G'dened is on very easy terms with his father, D'ram, and like him, mourns the death of Fanna. G'dened also tries hard to arbitrate between the two factions on Pern, but finds his own sympathies totally with the Benden Weyrleaders and their following.

107

Kylara

Found in Search from Telgar Weyr, Kylara is a full sister of the present Lord Holder, Larad. She is diametrically the opposite in looks, character and upbringing to Lessa. Fully sensual and accustomed to using her femininity to obtain her wishes, Kylara is a striking beauty—proud, haughty, with unusual blonde hair and a piercing eye.

Doted on by her father, the late Lord Holder, and indulged by her old nurse, Rannelly, Kylara had naturally assumed that she would be chosen by the one queen egg on the Hatching Ground. She was one of the first to arrive at Benden and, imperious by nature and education, tried to impose her will on those in the Lower Cavern, coming up hard against Manora's authority. When Lessa Impressed, Kylara went into a towering rage which Manora cooled by throwing a bucket of cold water on her.

Because Kylara was pregnant by an unidentifiable rider, custom also compelled Manora to keep the disruptive girl in the Weyr but even Manora's patience was strained by the arrogant beauty. Kylara demanded the right to stand on the Hatching Grounds a second time and, to everyone's amazement, Impressed Prideth.

For some time after that she was so bemused by being a queen rider that her behavior improved. But sensuality was aroused by the dragon's maturity and Kylara had no trouble luring anyone to her bed, though of them all T'bor was the most besotted.

For a while Kylara was nearly content to be Weyrwoman at Southern until she met Lord Meron of Nabol and recognized a fellow spirit, with a mutual aim—to destroy F'lar and Lessa. She became as obsessed with Meron as he with her and, quite by chance, took a fearful revenge on the Weyr. And on herself.

For Kylara had been far more bound to her Prideth than she could have realized and when her dragon went *between*, mortally wounded, the wrench broke Kylara's mind. Attended by her old nurse, Rannelly, Kylara existed, mindless and broken, in a small chamber at Fort Weyr.

Her setting is the light, airy room in the Southern Weyr which she has decorated with sensuous fabrics and the flowing draperies she preferred.

Felena

A good sort of person, but prone to gossip, Felena hopes to step into Manora's shoes, but at the same time is hoping she does not because she would never be sure she could really live up to Manora's standards. Well trained by the Head-woman, she nevertheless has occasional lapses of understanding. Felena is quite capable and basically kindhearted.

FELENA

©Robin Wood 1988

T'gellan

T'gellan epitomizes exactly the sort of vigorous young rider whom F'lar hoped to bring into the Weyr in his first Turns as Leader. With his black wavy hair, dark grey, penetrating eyes under level brows, and his angular face and frame, T'gellan exudes confidence and ability so it is not surprising he is a bronze rider and wingleader.

T'gellan also has an intuition which will prompt him to act where other seasoned riders might hesitate. He is as quick in his personal life and spends a good deal of time delving into matters not customarily the business of dragonriders. He is tactful, which makes him popular with holders, big and little.

He is also a compassionate and understanding man, kind to children and old aunties and uncles, and quite willing to sit by a friend's bedside to bear him company. Lessa frequently requests him for special assignments. Practically every unattached girl in the Weyr, and most of the girls in the Holds, have tried their wiles on him; he's willing to be caught, but not for long. He has his eye on someone who doesn't happen to notice that he's watching her.

T'GELLEN

© Robin Wood 1988

K'van

K'van is a tribute to my younger brother, Kevin McCaffrey, who was stricken with osteomyelitis at twelve years of age. Through seven years of hospitalizations, operations, casts, braces—until the advent of penicillin—he neither complained nor cried. It is that courage and fortitude I tried to celebrate in young Keevan.

Once K'van has Impressed Heth, he has the companion-consoler *par excellence* and, no longer bully-able, all of K'van's intelligence, courage, and spirit blossom. He becomes one of the more valorous bronze riders, and a wing leader, toward the end of that Pass. Utterly dependable, loyal, responsible, thoughtful and considerate with a wry, often droll wit, his brown eyes can often be very solemn and his expression inscrutable. But when he smiles or laughs, his humor is infectious, and can start a ripple of laughter throughout the Lower Cavern or a Gather.

K'VAN

© Robin Reed 1988

MORETA

A full thousand turns before the stories told in *Dragonflight*, the Harper Hall trilogy, and other novels of Pern, a young woman by the name of Moreta Impressed a golden dragon by the name of Orlith and became Weyrwoman at Fort Weyr.

Moreta was a talented veterinary surgeon, a talent which stood her in good stead during the tragedy which later became the subject matter for the harper ballad "Moreta's Ride"—which Menolly conducts during Threadfall.

A strange, fierce beast from Southern has been discovered by seamen from Ista Sea Hold floating in the Great Current—a feline. The joy of a gather on a balmy Pern day is quickly turned to bitter pain when first runnerbeasts and then humans are struck down by an unexpected, undiagnosed disease which quickly reaches plague proportions.

The books *Moreta: Dragonlady of Pern* and *Nerilka's Story* tell of the same event from different points of view. Here are the characters from the early days of Pern.

Moreta

Moreta is a woman in her late thirties, moving with purpose but at odds with much of her life, except for Orlith. She is that rarity on Pern, a blonde, her short, naturally waving curls streaked by the sun, her green eyes often shading to a grey when she's sad or very thoughtful, as she often is. Moreta has a womanly figure but trim from years of riding, with square, capable hands. Her face shows much character. She has a straight nose, a fine wide brow, a generous mouth, and a firm chin. She is passive—until she finally meets Alessan. That meeting polarizes all her unspoken, unfulfilled desires and makes her come alive for the first time since she was removed from her Hold on Search.

She is also the captive of her position in Pern society as Weyrwoman, as Weyr healer for the dragons, and mostly as Orlith's rider. She is all and more than any heroine should be and seldom is, and her tragedy is all the more poignant because she was so close to being a happy, active person.

It is perhaps ironic that she is posing here in flying gear, blonde curls framing her profile, with a typical Keroon holding in the background including the runner beasts of her childhood.

Alessan

There are people who must assume harder burdens than most and endure ordeals that would break lesser men. Be it stated that Alessan's youth was pleasant enough, for he had brothers to share his father's hard discipline and training, and sisters who adored him. Alessan is tall and well built, tending more to sinew than bulging muscle as suits a riding man. He has light green eyes, flecked with brown, and fair skin, emphasized by dark, slightly waving hair. His features are strong but tempered with a fineness inherited from his mother.

Reckless, and somewhat devious in his youth to evade Lord Leef's stringent requirements, Alessan is first sobered by his adored Suriana's death, then nearly overwhelmed by the epidemic which ruthlessly decimates family and Hold. Sheer perversity and then dogged determination *not* to accept defeat strengthen and sustain him. The loss of Moreta, for whom he has an inexplicable affinity, provides both reward and yet a third sorrow.

Alessan is a man for his time and demonstrates once again the resilience of the human spirit, surmounting all obstacles to survive and prosper.

Capiam

Masterhealer of Pern at a critical time in its healing history, the planet is to be greatly in his debt. As Alessan provides an example to the Holders, Capiam provides one to his Craft Hall. It is Pern's good fortune that Capiam is more flexible in his Craft than many of his recent predecessors. Certainly he is as obstinate as Alessan, looking for an answer to almost insoluble problems. He is willing to sacrifice his own life to provide an answer.

Totally dedicated to his Craft, Capiam's devotion is leavened by a whimsical sense of humor and strengthened by an infallible knowledge of his duty. He is in appearance an active man, though a stoop is beginning to alter his posture. He has thick, dark hair, dark eyes and a dark complexion which often give him a somber appearance, until he smiles, showing white and even teeth. His features are regular and strong, and generate an aura of assurance and competence of inestimable value to a healer.

Leri

Elder, and now retired, Weyrwoman of Fort Weyr in Moreta's time, and Moreta's best friend, Leri has seen it all! She struggles against a crippling joint-ail, eased by (perhaps) too liberal doses of fellis in her wine, but she misses little that goes on in the Weyr. She knows better than to give gratuitous advice but generally manages to convey it subtly, or through other spokespeople. She is biding her time, for she knows her usefulness is at an end. Although she could have retired to Ista Weyr, and enjoyed the warmth and the sun on her aching bones, she also knows that Moreta, though the young woman is unaware of it, needs an impartial and understanding friend. So she lingers at Fort Weyr.

Leri is tolerant of frailties but none too patient with fools. She has no sympathy for Sh'gall but knows that he's the best leader the Weyr could have during the rest of this Pass. She wishes the best for Moreta, if that does not conflict with what is good for Fort Weyr and dragonriders. As many did, Leri valiantly rouses herself to great efforts during the epidemic, in effect sacrificing her dragon and herself. It is tragic that, in feeling confident of Moreta's abilities, she forgets Holth's habits, and Moreta fails to compensate for riding another's dragon.

Nerilka

Quite aware of her own unattractiveness and restricted by her father's pompous discipline, Nerilka finds the courage to leave Fort Hold when she overhears Lord Tolocamp's outrageous denial of Harper and Healer Hall requests. Discarding rank and safety, she sets out to become useful in a society that is in great confusion and distress.

Tall, thin, dark haired, with fair but tanned skin and hazel eyes, Nerilka has few of the affectations of her father and brother, none of the narrow views of her mother, and a desperate need to serve. Remarkably enough, she finds the best place on all Pern in which to serve and, patient, tolerant, understanding, she fills the one role she never expected to enjoy. The hills receding in the mists behind her symbolize her own emergence from nonentity.

B'lerion

Known as a stealer of hearts, B'lerion is the rider of bronze Nabeth, and enjoys all the perquisites of his station. He is tall and lean, with blue eyes, sun-streaked hair, and a square, weathered face. B'lerion has a genuine charm of manner, a wry sense of humor and, when required, an infallible way of dealing with people and emergencies. He is young enough to risk much on the moment and take the consequences.

Unaccountably smitten by the shy graces of Oklina, he presses his advantage and makes certain she Impresses.

B'LERION

©Robin Wood 1988

Campen

Campen is a younger version of his father, but without the authority of experience or independent thought. He follows the path of least resistance and obeys. He frets constantly and wants to be allowed to prove himself. In his father's absence, he thinks that he has, though it is Nerilka who initiates any variation from Fort Hold order.

CAMPEN

© Robin Wood 1988

Dag and Fergal

Dag is small, barrel-chested, and spindle-legged. He has big hands and a big heart. His manner is gruff, but he is a dab hand with the runner beasts. He connives on his own and for young Alessan, who shares his great love of the fleet runners they secretly breed. He is also, though he wouldn't admit it, Alessan's closest friend and admirer.

Fergal, his grandson, has taken a page from Dag's book without either the Turns or experience, but with a great deal of instinctive wisdom with beasts. He is small, wiry, acrobatic, caustic, and crafty. He is at the age of adolescent rebellion and belligerence, but devoted to his grandfather. He barely tolerates Alessan, is suspicious of Rill (Nerilka's nickname) and will only obey Oklina, whom he secretly adores.

DAG
& FERGAL

© Robin Wood 1988

Desdra

Desdra is not a big person physically, but she is possessed of so much personality that she seems larger than she is. Her features are not pretty, but her brown eyes sparkle with inner amusements and reflections.

A more-than-competent healer and dedicated to her Craft, she is surprised by her unexpected attachment to Master Capiam, deciding at long last that she can be both Healer and Wife, since it is plain that Capiam would neglect himself without supervision.

DESDRA

© Robin Wood 1988

K'lon

The first Weyr victim of the influenza, K'lon, rider of blue Rogeth, is also a catalyst in his position on Pern, though he'd be the last to realize it. Of medium height, with sun-bleached, mid-brown hair and blue eyes, he is an attractive man in his mid-thirties. He is a good dragonrider, a good friend, and a thoughtful person, given to considerable internal speculation. He frets a good deal about minor details, not wishing to disappoint or annoy, and at times lends too much importance to the opinions of others. He has instinctive good taste and a very agreeable manner. But he has a friendly smile that often attracts confidences he would rather not hear. Because he survived the dreaded plague, he is also obsessed with a sense of guilt for surviving.

K'LON

©Robin Wood 1988

Lord Ratoshigan

If one gathered together all the despicable, undesirable meanness that a Lord Holder could possess in one small frame, you'd end up with Lord Ratoshigan. Perhaps it has to do with his lack of stature, but Ratoshigan is determined to have everything his way and anything he wants before anyone else has a chance at it. He cares about himself first, last, and always. Always immaculately attired to show off his miniature perfections, he never gives an inch. He has no friends: only minions, servile and uncomplaining.

If justice were meted out, he should never have been made Lord Holder, nor should he have survived the plague. But he's the sort that would.

RATOSHIGAN

© Robin Wood 1988

Oklina

A slight girl who adores her older brother, Alessan, Oklina is the youngest of the Ruathan brood and, as such, the last one to be considered by busy adults. Accepting this, Oklina is one of those sensitive, caring people whose unassuming gracefulness can ease and charm. It is this quality that first attracts the carefree B'lerion. Not pretty in the usual way, Oklina has wide-set, deep eyes, a short, cute nose, and a wide, sensitive mouth. She is as quick to be merry as to be sorrowful, and she has a lot of that in her life. Her quality of uncritical caring makes her an unexpectedly satisfying companion. She is fiercely loyal, tenacious in any purpose in her own quiet, self-effacing way, and the sort who will throw herself wholeheartedly into any project.

OKLINA

©Robin Wood 1988

141.

Sh'gall

A clever warrior and a fearless leader in the constant battle against Thread, Sh'gall is a complex personality, uneasy with himself and those around him. All the qualities that make him a superb Weyrleader mitigate against him in other areas. He is tall and attractive though a sullen expression and an innately suspicious nature detract from the first impression that here is the apotheosis of a dedicated dragonrider. That he is, but he lacks a human touch, much humor, or any real insight into other people's problems and emotions. He is sometimes deliberately ambiguous, giving people opportunities to disobey or misunderstand him so he has a chance to wield his authority as Weyrleader. His riders endure his irascibility because they grudgingly admit his infallibility as a strategist against Thread and would follow his orders in the air implicitly.

Sh'gall is also frustrated on several levels, in a subconscious recognition that he doesn't have the light and easy manner that L'mal had; in his association with Moreta because he senses that she has no real emotional involvement with him beyond their dragons' needs; and in his knowledge that all too soon his usefulness and prestige will end, with the cessation of this Fall.

SH'GALL

©Robin Wood 1988

Master Tirone

A handsome enough man, tall and well proportioned, with a better-than-average voice, Tirone is a master of assessing situations and reacting positively. He is an opportunist, perhaps, but as Masterharper he has an unenviable role in many ways. He enjoys his prestige and is generally quite candid and fair in his dealings. He can afford to be. In repose, his face is rather sad, but no one has ever learned what occasioned this. Generally he is bombastic, jovial, forceful, and able to plow through most objections, merely by the volume of his carrying voice.

TIRONE

© Robin Wood 1988

Lord Tolocamp

He is the sort of man whom you want to shake out of his complacency, rub his nose in what he cannot see for looking, or cudgel him into submission. Tolocamp is an infuriating man because he must *always* be right. Jovial when not contradicted and in the normal run of events, Tolocamp is a capable if unimaginative Holder, convinced of his moral rectitude and infinite wisdom. His weakness is pretty women, which no longer describes his wife, Lady Pendra. He feels considerable distaste for his unattractive daughters and is certain their plainness comes from his wife's Bloodline. He has forced his older sons into his mold by sheer willpower and never does recover from his daughter Nerilka's astonishing defection.

LORD TOLOCAMP

©Robin Wood 1988

Feline

The feline which brought plague from the southern continent was the size of a well-developed lynx, with the "clouded" markings of one of its genetic forebears. Captured in a weakened state by sailors who were replenishing water and fresh foods on the peninsula (originally called the Delta Province and later named Southern Hold), the beast is a descendant of animals regenerated for the purpose of combating the larger and more vicious tunnel snakes, whose depredations caused the original settlers such problems.

The "cats" survived the earthquake which freed them from captivity, then proliferated on the southern continent. But they carried the dormant virus that could flare into plague. Their numbers were often reduced by outbreaks of disease.

FELINE FROM SOUTHERN CONTINENT

©Robin Wood 1988

A Guide To Pern

ABUNA	DRAGONSINGER	KITCHEN	HARPER HALL
ALEMI	DRAGONSONG	FISHER	HALF-CIRCLE SEAHOLD
ALESSAN	MORETA	LORD HOLDER	RUATHA HOLD
AMANIA	DRAGONSINGER	CRAFTER	HARPER HALL
ARNOR	DRAGONSINGER	MASTER	HARPER HALL
AUDIVA	DRAGONSINGER	CRAFTER	HARPER HALL
B'LERION—NABETH	MORETA	RIDER	HIGH REACHES WEYR
BRAND	WHITE DRAGON	HOLDER	RUATHA HOLD
BREKKE—WIRENTH	DRAGONQUEST	RIDER	BENDEN WEYR
BRIALA	DRAGONSINGER	CRAFTER	HARPER HALL
BROLLY	DRAGONSINGER	APPRENTICE	HARPER HALL
BRUDEGAN	DRAGONSINGER	JOURNEYMAN	HARPER HALL
CAMO	DRAGONSINGER	KITCHEN	HARPER HALL
CAMPEN	MORETA	HOLDER	FORT HOLD
CORANA	WHITE DRAGON	HOLDER	RUATHA
DAG	MORETA	BEASTMAN	RUATHA HOLD
DEELAN	WHITE DRAGON	WETNURSE	RUATHA HOLD
DESDRA	MORETA	HEALER	FORT HEALER HALL
DOMICK (MASTER)	DRAGONSINGER	COMPOSER	HARPER HALL
DORSE	WHITE DRAGON	MILKBROTHER	RUATHA HALL
DUNCA	DRAGONSINGER	COTKEEPER	FORT HOLD
ELGION	DRAGONSONG	JOURNEYMAN	HALF CIRCLE SEAHOLD
F'LAR—MNEMENTH	DRAGONFLIGHT	WEYRLEADER	BENDEN WEYR
F'LESSAN—GOLANTH	WHITE DRAGON	RIDER	BENDEN WEYR
F'NOR—CANTH	DRAGONFLIGHT	WINGSECOND	BENDEN WEYR
FANDAREL	DRAGONFLIGHT	MASTERSMITH	TELGAR
FAX (LORD)	DRAGONFLIGHT	LORD HOLDER	HIGH REACHES HOLD
FELENA	DRAGONFLIGHT	WEYR COOK	BENDEN WEYR
FELINE	MORETA	ANIMAL	SOUTHERN
FERGAL	MORETA	APPRENTICE	RUATHA HOLD
G'DENED—BARANTH	DRAGONQUEST	WEYRLEADER	ISTA WEYR
GEMMA (LADY)	DRAGONFLIGHT	LADY HOLDER	HIGH REACHES HOLD
GROGHE (LORD)	DRAGONFLIGHT	LORD HOLDER	FORT HOLD
JAXOM—RUTH	DRAGONFLIGHT	LORD HOLDER	RUATHA HOLD
JERINT (MASTER)	DRAGONSINGER	CRAFTMASTER	HARPER HALL

K'LON—ROGETH	MORETA	RIDER	FORT WEYR
K'VAN—HETH	SMALLEST D'BOY	RIDER	BENDEN WEYR
KAYLA	DRAGONSINGER	KITCHEN	HARPER HALL
KYLARA—PRIDETH	DRAGONFLIGHT	WEYRWOMAN	SOUTHERN WEYR
LERI—HOLTH	MORETA	WEYRWOMAN	FORT WEYR—RETIRED
LESSA—RAMOTH	DRAGONFLIGHT	WEYRWOMAN	BENDEN WEYR
LYTOL—EX-LARTH	DRAGONFLIGHT	RIDER	BENDEN WEYR
MANORA	DRAGONFLIGHT	HEADWOMAN	BENDEN WEYR
MENOLLY	DRAGONSONG	HARPER	HALF CIRCLE SEAHOLD
MIRRIM	DRAGONQUEST	RIDER	BENDEN WEYR
MORETA—ORLITH	MORETA	WEYRWOMAN	FORT WEYR
MORSHAL (MASTER)	DRAGONSINGER	MASTER	HARPER HALL
N'TON—LIOTH	DRAGONQUEST	WEYRLEADER	FORT WEYR
NERILKA	MORETA/NERILKA	HOLDER	FORT HOLD
OKLINA	MORETA	HOLDER	RUATHA HOLD
OLDIVE (MASTER)	DRAGONSINGER	HEALER	FORT HEALER HALL
PETIRON (MASTER)	DRAGONSONG	HARPER	HALF CIRCLE SEAHOLD
PIEMUR	DRAGONSINGER	APPRENTICE	HARPER HALL
PONA	DRAGONSINGER	HOLDER	SOUTHERN BOLL HOLD
RANLY	DRAGONSINGER	APPRENTICE	HARPER HALL
RATOSHIGAN	MORETA	LORD HOLDER	SOUTHERN BOLL HOLD
ROBINTON (MASTER)	DRAGONFLIGHT	MASTERHARPER	HARPER HALL
SEBELL (MASTER)	DRAGONSINGER	MASTER	HARPER HALL
SH'GALL—KADITH	MORETA	WEYRLEADER	FORT WEYR
SHARRA	WHITE DRAGON	HEALER	SOUTHERN HOLD
SHONAGAR (MASTER)	DRAGONSINGER	VOICEMASTER	SOUTHERN HOLD
SILVINA	DRAGONSINGER	HEADWOMAN	HARPER HALL
T'GELLAN—MONARTH	DRAGONSONG	WINGLEADER	BENDEN WEYR
TALMOR	DRAGONSINGER	JOURNEYMAN	HARPER HALL
TERRY (MASTER)	DRAGONFLIGHT	SMITHMASTER	TELGAR HOLD
TIRONE (MASTER)	MORETA	MASTERHARPER	HARPER HALL
TOLOCAMP (LORD)	MORETA	LORD HOLDER	FORT HOLD
TORIC (SELF-STYLED LORD)	WHITE DRAGON	HOLDER	SOUTHERN HOLD
WANSOR (MASTER)	DRAGONQUEST	GLASSMASTER	SMITHCRAFT HALL
YANUS (LORD)	DRAGONSONG	LORD HOLDER	HALF CIRCLE SEAHOLD